Reader's Clubhouse

DOC BLOCK

By David F. Marx
Illustrated by Matt Phillips

BARRON'S

Table of Contents

Illustrations on pages 21–23 created by Carol Stutz

All inquiries should be addressed to:
Barron's Educational Series, Inc.
250 Wireless Boulevard
Hauppauge, New York 11788
www.barronseduc.com

Library of Congress Catalog Card No.: 2005053584

ISBN-13: 978-0-7641-3288-9
ISBN-10: 0-7641-3288-1

Library of Congress Cataloging-in-Publication Data
Marx, David F.
    Doc Block / David F. Marx.
        p. cm. – (Reader's clubhouse)
    ISBN-13: 978-0-7641-3288-9
    ISBN-10: 0-7641-3288-1
    1. Zoo animals—Juvenile literature. I. Title. II. Series.

QL77.5.M42 2006
590.73—dc22

                                                                                    2005053584

PRINTED IN CHINA
9 8 7 6 5 4 3 2 1

Dear Parent and Educator,

Welcome to the Barron's Reader's Clubhouse, a series of books that provide a phonics approach to reading.

Phonics is the relationship between letters and sounds. It is a system that teaches children that letters have specific sounds. Level 1 books introduce the short-vowel sounds. Level 2 books progress to the long-vowel sounds. This progression matches how phonics is taught in many classrooms.

Doc Block reviews the short "i," "o," and "u" sounds introduced in previous Level 1 books. Simple words with these short-vowel sounds are called **decodable words.** The child knows how to sound out these words because he or she has learned the sounds they include. This story also contains **high-frequency words.** These are common, everyday words that the child learns to read by sight. High-frequency words help ensure fluency and comprehension. **Challenging words** go a little beyond the reading level. The child will identify these words with help from the illustration on the page. All words are listed by their category on page 24.

Here are some coaching and prompting statements you can use to help a young reader read *Doc Block:*

- **On page 4, "Doc" is a decodable word. Point to the word and say:**

  Read this word. How did you know the word? What sounds did it make?

  Note: There are many opportunities to repeat the above instruction throughout the book.

- **On page 6, "croc" is a challenging word. Point to the word and say:**

  Read this word. It rhymes with "Doc." How did you know the word? Did you look at the picture? How did it help?

You'll find more coaching ideas on the Reader's Clubhouse Web site: *www.barronsclubhouse.com.* Reader's Clubhouse is designed to teach and reinforce reading skills in a fun way. We hope you enjoy helping children discover their love of reading!

Sincerely,

Nancy Harris

Nancy Harris
Reading Consultant

This is Doc Block.

He can fix a lot.

A croc is on a rock.

Call on Doc.
He can fix the croc.

A hog is lost in a fog.

Call on Doc.
He can fix the hog.

A chimp got a limp.

Call on Doc.
He can fix the chimp.

A skunk is in a funk.

Call on Doc.
He can fix the skunk.

A duck is stuck.

Call on Doc.
He can fix the duck.

Doc Block can see a clock.

It is six. He must stop.

Doc Block can fix a lot.

Fun Facts About
Zoos

- The largest zoo in the United States is the North Carolina Zoo. It is about the size of 500 football fields!

- The National Zoo in Washington, D.C., is home to more than 2,700 animals. The zoo's most famous resident is the giant panda from China.

- African elephants at the zoo in Knoxville, Tennessee, are artists. They paint with their trunks. Their paintings have sold for as much as $1,350!

- Zoo animals live in different enclosures that are similar to the animals' habitats in the wild. Here are a few examples of enclosures you might see in your local zoo (see next page).

Bird habitat

Aquarium
(fish, dolphins, turtles,
and others)

Land habitat
(bears, lions, giraffes,
and others)

Jungle habitat
(monkeys, gorillas,
orangutans, and others)

Make an Animal Mask

You will need:

- paper plates
- non-toxic paints or markers
- elastic or string
- tape or stapler
- decorations for your mask (feathers, construction paper, pipe cleaners, etc.)
- safety scissors

1. Draw a pencil outline of your animal's eyes, nose, and mouth on a plate. You will be cutting out the eyes to see through, so make sure they are big enough.

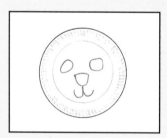

Front View

2. Use another paper plate to draw the shape of your animal's ears. Cut out your shapes using safety scissors. Using tape or a stapler, attach the ears to the mask.

3. Attach a piece of elastic or string to each side of your mask so it fits around the back of your head.

Back View

4. Color or paint your mask to look like your animal.

Word List

Challenging Words	Block chimp clock	croc skunk stuck
Short I, O, U Decodable Words	Doc duck fix fog funk got hog limp lost	lot must rock six stop
High-Frequency Words	a call can he in is it on see the this	